Paper Girls 6

BRIAN K. VAUGHAN writer
CLIFF CHIANG artist
MATT WILSON colors
JARED K. FLETCHER letters

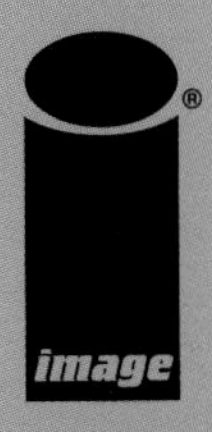

Image Comics, INC.

Robert Kirkman - Chief Operating Officer
Erik Larsen - Chief Financial Officer
Todd McFarlane - President
Marc Silvestri - Chief Executive Officer
Jim Valentino - Vice President

Eric Stephenson - Publisher / Chief Creative Officer
Jeff Boison - Director of Publishing Planning & Book Trade Sales
Chris Ross - Director of Digital Sales
Jeff Stang - Director of Specialty Sales
Kat Salazar - Director of PR & Marketing
Drew Gill - Art Director
Heather Doornink - Production Director
Nicole Lapalme - Controller

IMAGECOMICS.COM

Dee Cunniffe - Color Flats
Jared K. Fletcher - Logo + Book Design

PAPER GIRLS, VOLUME 6. First Printing. September 2019. Published by Image Comics, Inc. Office of publication: 2701 NW Vaughn St., Suite 780, Portland, OR 97210.

ISBN 978-1-5343-1324-8

APPLE PIE
APPLE PIE
THE BODY OF CHRIST!
Wait.
You want me to eat this?
Does it get me kicked out of paradise... or invited in?
Damn, remember when those things used to be fried?
APPLE PIE

In the future, they're gonna be baked.
And they *suck.*
APPLE PIE
APPLE PIE

Missy.
How do you know about the *future?*
Sorry, Mom says I'm not supposed to talk about stuff that makes you anxious.

So I'll just put you out of your mis

8888888888

My hero.

Don't get too attached, new kid.
Turns out I'm not the man you think I am.

Now listen up, I came all this way to tell you something important.
If you want to get back home, you have to **moonwalk,** understand?

This is a dream.
This is a dream and I totally know that I'm dreaming.
No, this is a **message,** and if you forget...

...we're all gonna burn in **hell.**

hhht
AHHH!
It's okay, Erin.
You're safe now.

What is this?
How do you know my *name?!*
RIP

My son said you ***fainted.***
And we found your "A.N.D.G." card.

Whoa.
I didn't even know they still ***made*** those.
THE AMERICAN NEWSPAPER DELIVERY GUILD
SINCE 1899!
MEMBERSHIP CARD
Erin Tieng
YOUR NAME
3905137
MEMBER ID

Where's your squad?
My what?
Your friends. You trick-or-treating ***alone?***
No. I...I don't know. There was some kind of ***explosion*** and--
Dad!

The sky is all wrong!

...moonwalk...

POP
Umm, what just happened?

Sorry, Grand Father.
We left 002016 at our usual trajectory, but we seem to have been waylaid.
In what bloody year?
That's the thing, sir.
We're not in a specific time, we're... interstitial.
We're *inside* the fourth dimension?
Well, "inside" is a relative term, but--
How the devil do we get out?
According to the last transmission we were able to receive from back home, our Main Folding seems to have been **closed.**
By what?
By whom, actually.

Five youths, but that's all I can tell you.
Instruments weren't even able to detect their basic vitals, much less make any positive identifications, though a few of them seem...familiar.
Cardinal, what if this is them?
The four girls we lost in '88.
What if we all just passed each other?
Some of their garb matches the era.
But what about this one? She's dressed more like one of our shitty descendants.
And if an enemy fighter found these poor kids before us...
Did...did that animal just murder innocent civilians?
Worse, she weaponized them.
I don't follow.
By scattering these girls to different corners of the hypercube, she didn't just bend a single year inside itself, she--
RUVRUV RUUVV

That's...
not one of
ours.
Breach!
Huh.
Grand Father,
all hands are
struggling just to
batten down the
Cathedral.
We're in no
shape to repel
invaders!
Yeah, well,
the future is
never fair.
Just
inevitable.

Awesome.

Where the hell am I this time?
Did you fellas hear that?
The girl, she...she *cussed*.

1958?
Guess it could have been worse.
Right over there.

I heard 'em lighting off *fireworks*.

There another way out?
Um, sure.
You in some kind of trouble?

Not yet.
But Cleveland P.D. isn't big on asking questions first.

Amen.
Goose it, you two.
We'll give 'em the runaround.

Glorious afternoon, officers!
Where'd you come from, anyway?
I heard a ***bang,*** and then you was just standing there, looking like you stepped out of the *Flash Gordon* funnies.

That's it.

That's what?

Do you know if The Preserver has started running a strip called, like, Freddy Potato?
Frankie Tomatah?
Yeah, it's two down from Brick Bradford, why?

I have to find the guy who draws it.
His daughter, more importantly.
Well, I doubt a guy that famous has got a listed number.

But I could maybe help you out...

...long as you give me those swell boots.

Are you fucking kidding me?

Stay back!
Lay a finger on me, I bring this *sap* down on your pretty--

NAH!

Hey!

You want a new pair of shoes, get back on your bike and sling papers.
But if I ever hear you tried to rob another kid, I'm going to find you and kick your teeth out of your face, understood?
Who... who *are* you?

Still figuring that out.

AAHHH!

...KJ...

I know you.

You're...you're the lady who invented *time travel.*
Haven't been called that in a long time.
Mac, isn't it?

But, I thought you and your friends all made it *home.*
When I finally got back to the late 21st century, the first thing I did was dig up what happened to... to each of you.

So you know *my* fairy tale ending, huh?
Yeah, first I heard it was gonna be leukemia, but according to a dickhole's second opinion, it's something called *4DC.*

Sweetheart, I'm so sorry.
I swear, I had no idea we'd have to pay so much for all this.
"We"?

They didn't realize when I was diagnosed either, but I'm Patient Zero of the same disease *you* regrettably contracted.
That's why I came here, to die with the rest of our planet.

Uh, about that second part...
In thirty-eight minutes, a gamma-ray burst from a nearby galaxy is going to permanently extinguish all life on Earth, just shy of her five billionth birthday.
And you came here by *choice?*

I didn't want Wari and Jahpo to have to deal with my ***remains,*** so when my health took a turn, I dug up my old Beta Model for one last trip.
Maybe it's cheating, but I thought it would be cool to hang on until the finish line, you know? To run the whole...

Forgive me, my manners are disappearing with the rest of my mind.
Qanta Braunstein, excellent-if-baffling to see you again.

Are you ***all right?*** How in the world did you end up ***here?***
I heard a strange noise--stranger than usual, anyway--and ran to investigate and... whatever, please, just tell me everything you can remember.

I kissed a girl.

Oh.

Tiffany Quilkin!

I've been waiting my whole life to meet you.

This is *your* fault!

RAHHHH!
Now just a--

Uhnf!

What did you do to my friends?!
That wasn't me!
It was one of my...my *predecessors!*

Bitch, what are you *talking* about?!

Please, just hear me out.
It was the ***first*** genetic duplicate of Erin Tieng who detonated the device that brought you here.

Her generation was a lot...angrier than mine.

Still, if it wasn't for those pioneers, we never would have ended the war.
With the old-timers.
The war...?

It's finally over.

Welcome to a harmonious utopia of complete global peace.
Can I get you some hot chocolate?

If your side were really the good guys, why did I just get **blown up?**
You didn't.
You were safely transported thousands of years in your future. So you could **help** us.

Help you do what?

End the war, of course.

But, you just said--
Tiffany, we're the good guys because our side never stopped believing that a fairer, more just world was possible for everyone.

Unlike the old-timers, we still have hope.

We still have dreams.

“Rule #4: A paperboy is always clean in appearance, dress and spirit.”

–From *The American Newspaper Delivery Guild Handbook,* published in 1932

All clear.
It's safe for you to come out now.

About goddamn time.

You're a lifesaver, Charlotte.
Literary.
I think you mean "literally."
Sorry.
That's what I get for dropping Oldenglish my sophomore year.
Oh, Jude, are you sure you can't stay just a little longer?
I...I wish I could, but I have to get back to my friends, see if they've made any progress with our ship.
But you promise you'll let me see it? Your time machine?
Charlotte!
What the heck is wrong with the set?
The Real McCoys is about to start!
Uh-oh.

Go to your father, my dear.
I'll meet you back here tomorrow night.
You promise?

I swear.
The future still needs your help.

Hey, Jude.

VMMMMMMMM
Don't make it bad.

Yeah, I don't know what that means, but if you make any sudden moves, I'm gonna dropkick your face off.

You work for the old-timers?
Hardly.
I'm just a regular old ***kid*** trying to get home to 1988. That's where I met your buddies Heck and Naldo.

'88?
What the were we doing in that mess?

Beats me, but it started with you rolling my friend Tiffany for one of her pricey Radio Shack walkies.
Wait, not a TRC-218?
With channel 14 crystals?!

Huh?

My guys and I are like one of your old super-gods, **Robyne Hude.**
We steal from the greedy past to give to our needy present, dig?

Whatever, can you get me back to my girlfriend or not?

Your...?
I mean, we're not "official" or anything.
But we probably will be, ***if*** you let me tag along.

Respect, kid.
I was still in the closet at your age, and my people actually ***like*** our kind.

Guess your era's way cooler than the history books say.

This hike... would be a lot easier...with a Camel Light... or twenty...
No time for vices, Mac.
We have to get you inside my capsule before ***the end.***

But, why can't you come ***with*** me?
Who says you have to die in some radioactive apocalypse with a bunch of disgusting monsters?
They're not monsters, they're the fittest survivors of billions of years of ***evolution,*** and some of the most beautiful creatures ever to walk our--

KAROOM

DOC!

My weapon!
Use it!

I'm trying!
Stupid thing's not working!
klik klik

iBeam!
Safety off, for Christ's sake!

Okay.
Hang on to your--

KRACK

UNF!

That was *hnn* badass.
You all right?
Sounded like you **broke** something.

Just my brother's old Walkman.
And the last thing I dubbed off him, probably.

Huh, my **father** used to have one much like this.
Your father?
Hey, why don't we just go back to **his** time, tell your younger self never to invent any of this crap?

I wish that were a possibility, but unfortunately, the world is like one of **these**.

You lost me, Braunstein.
Time, it's not unlike your *cassette.*
It's comprised of one long spool, stretching from beginning to end, and each segment can only be recorded over so many times before it begins to *degrade.*

But, I'm not talking about erasing, like, all of human history!
Let's just go back and make sure that neither of us catch the shitty time-travel disease that's gonna do us both in!

I've tried, actually, but turns out that death is not unlike breaking the little *tab* off of one of these things.
Maybe it's God's way of making sure that His designs can only be changed so much.

Hold on.
You're saying God is *real?*

I know, when I was your age, I always *hated* when people ascribed whatever they didn't fully understand to some mythical being.
But the older I've gotten, the more I've come to believe that there must be *some* kind of higher power at work out there.

What kind of asshole creator would let a *kid* die?

You have every right to be pissed, Mac.
Nothing about life is fair...but at least yours isn't over yet.
So what? Even if I escape this nightmare, I have what, a few more years left, tops?

I know this will sound strange coming from someone in my line of work, but the amount of *time* we're each given is irrelevant.

It's what we choose to *do* with every second that counts.

Anyway, at least your tape survived.
Is it a good one?
Nah.

It's the fucking best.

What the eff is even happening right now?

Tiffany, this is my fellow genetic duplicate of Erin Tieng.
She's seven years older... if not always wiser.
Sup.

And you may recognize your friend ***KJ*** in this more distinguished clone of--
You.
You're... you're a copy of ***me,*** aren't you?

No, sweetheart.
I ***am*** you.

Say what now?
It's me, "Double-Oh Tiff"!
I'm the same older version of us you saved from my train wreck of a life back in 2000!

That... that isn't possible.
Hmmm, how can I prove it to you?
Well, remember third grade? When we shoplifted that pack of Garbage Pail Kids without getting caught? We've never confessed that to ***anyone,*** not even--

But, I watched you ***explode!*** And...and how you die is how you die!

True, but it only ***looked*** as if I perished.
Sixty years ago, people from this glorious paradise swooped in a split second before that blast to transport me to their time. They *Freejack-ed* me!

Who the hell is Free Jack?

Was that not out in '88?
Thought for sure I'd seen that when we were your age.

Tiffany, our foremothers rescued your older self for the same reason they gave birth to us: because you and each of your friends are vitally important to the future.

If that's true, where's ***Mac?***

Look, "it's complicated" is the understatement of the friggin' mega-annum.
But all you need to know is that these ladies and I are gonna reunite you with ***all three*** of your fellow papergirls.

Then why haven't you done it already?
Because we still need your assistance.
The only way our monstrous war--any war, really--finally ends is by opening up ***lines of communication.***

Back in the day, to talk across the ages, these folks would rely on coded letters left in newspapers by allies like the cartoonist woman you met.
But the old-timers eventually figured out that trick.

So we had to get a little more ***creative*** to send stuff they could never intercept.

Building off the brain-machine interface of ancient gadgets like this one, we invented a way to narrowcast transmissions directly into unconscious minds in the past.

Dreams.
Our dreams are secret messages from the ***future.***

Told you I was a smart cookie.
But here's how it crumbles.
We've discovered that our creation works most clearly with one's ***contemporaries.***

All of us have tried talking to your pals, but not even Senior Citizen You can make a strong enough connection.
Which is where ***12-Year-Old You*** comes in.

You're the one person here who can break through to your crew.
We need you to reach out to as many as you can, and help guide them into position for a plan that will ultimately create peace on Earth.
P

This is totally bonkers.
What makes you guys think any of this is really going to work?

That's the thing, beautiful.

It already has.

Don't wuss out now, Erin.

The dream told you to moonwalk, right?
I think that means I have to *retrace my steps...*

...back to where this all started.
FORECLOSURE
FOR SALE

NO TRESPASSING!
BANK OWNED PROPERTY
direct call

Tiffany?
Anyone...?

Can't believe I'm doing this ***again.***

Um.
Hello?

Please.
I don't know what you want, but I'm just looking for something my friends and I found down here a few days...I mean, *years* ago.

Quit messing around.
I *know* this is where I'm supposed to be. I had, like, a...

...vision?
FUCK

Yecch.
Boys are the *worst*.

Ahh!
RUV
RUV
RUUUVVV

God.
Oh, God.

You can do this, dummy.
Your family, your ***friends***, everyone you love is on the other side of that thing.

It's like Mr. T says, "You gotta follow your dreams."
Just follow your...

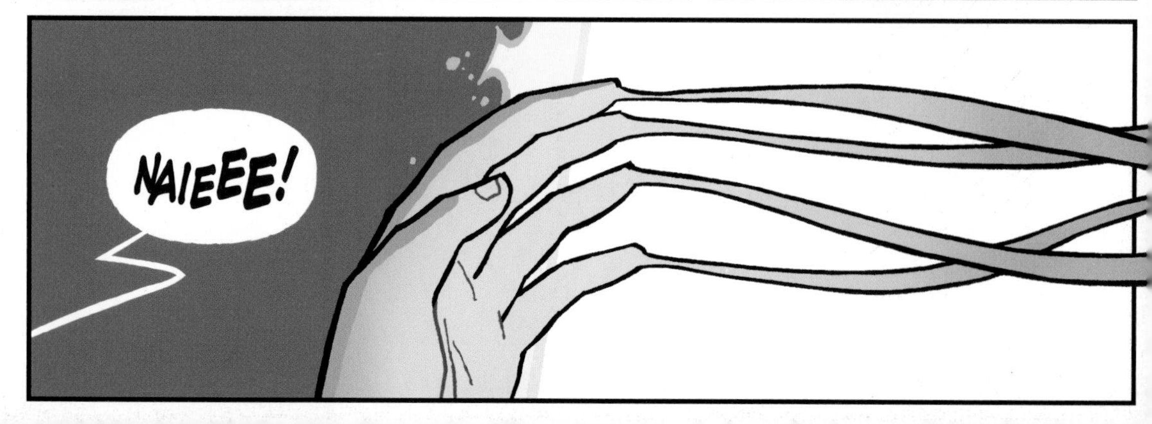
NAIEEE!

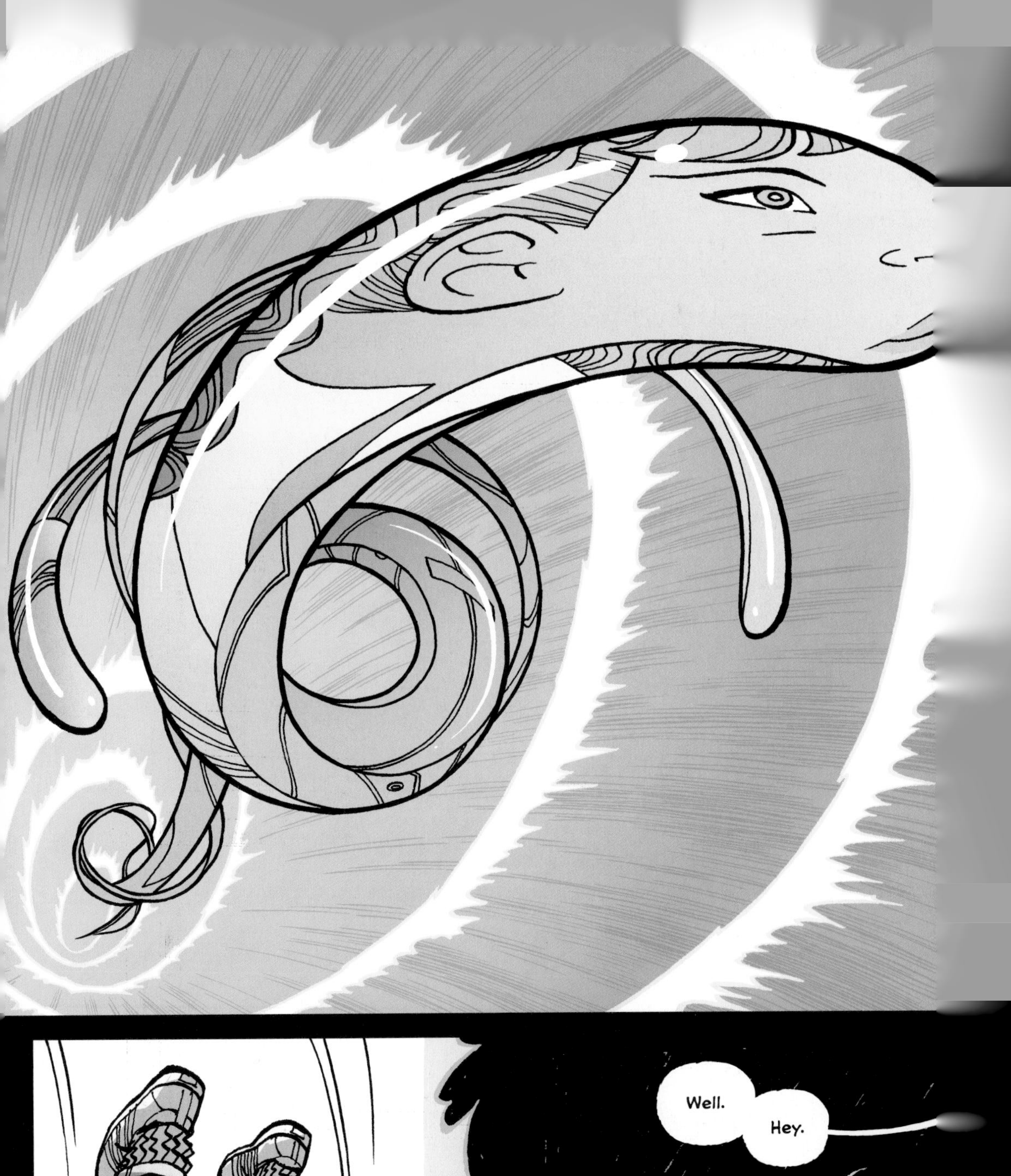

OOHF!
Well.
Hey.

Awesome to finally make your acquaintance.

“Rule #3: A paperboy sticks to his route, from start to finish.”

–From *The American Newspaper Delivery Guild Handbook,* published in 1932

Why
are
we
here?

Now there's a question old as time.
I like to think it's *fate.*
Who gives a shit?
Philosophers don't last long in my line of work.
I was rather hoping *you* could tell us why we've ended up in this great beyond, Miss...?

No.
No way.
I don't have to tell you old-timers *anything.*

Believe it or not, Tiffany, "here" is actually your old neighborhood.
Though these days, it's way more Stream than Stony.
This entire sector frequently overlaps with the kind of fissures in four-dimensional space that allow us to communicate with other eras.
No offense, but that doesn't sound very scientific.
Is fate really all that different than Einstein's determinism?
Sure, maybe you and your friends just happened to stumble onto that time machine, but I like to think the universe needed it to happen.
No, Jude, I mean, why did you drag me to Edgewater, where the acne crowd goes to lock braces?
Oh, when our "lifeboat" arrived in '58, it splashed down in your filthy lake, so my and I set up camp not far from here.
Careful making your way down...
Grand Father, she's carrying the same satchel as the young ones who attacked me in 001988!
This poor girl's not our enemy, she's just an innocent bystander...isn't that right?

So wherever Erin, Mac, and KJ ended up, Old Sparky here is really going to let me *talk* to them? When they're *asleep?*
And the message we need you to deliver is this: ***return to the beginning.***
Typically during their last period of R.E.M.
In the end, what's it matter?
Life existed on this rock for less than a blink of the universe's eye, and somehow, against truly astronomical odds, you and I both got to be part of it!
Man, for a terminal cancer patient, you're like a living Bobby McFerrin song.
Heck and Naldo are probably still out scavenging for parts, but they should be back soon.
Cool, it'd be good to see some familiar faces.
Yeah, you said you met the two of them...but what about *me?*
Please, I just want to see my friends again.
And I give you my word we'll do everything in our power to make that happen.
For now, would you like to see our dinosaurs?

What does that *mean?*
At least one of your gal pals needs to find her way back to the same co-ordinates where you four first stumbled onto our forefathers' time machine.
But try to keep it simple. We've found that communiques sent this way tend to get a little *Freddy Krueger-ed* as they pass through the subconscious.
Afraid I don't understand the reference.
Right.
Before your time.
Uhhhhhm.
Save me the old "can't know your own future" speech, KJ!
If something awful is gonna happen to me, I deserve to hear about it!
Did you say...?
I gather you've been introduced to our teenaged opponents?
They've likely told you that we're terribly dogmatic about altering the past, but I assure you that's not the case.

I realize I'm biased, but why don't we start with Erin Tieng?
Just concentrate on her memory, and keep repeating the dispatch in your mind.
I'm trying, but nothing seems to be...
HNN.
Doc?
You okay?
I'm so sorry.
But I think you die.
Years ago, we learned you could rescue majestic creatures like these from moments before a comet strike, for example, and not alter the history of our planet one precious butterfly flap.
But our descendants have shown a reckless disregard for--
Sorry, do you feel that... tingling?

What the eff was that?!
Just a...a 4D fault line back to somewhere in the Paleocene Era, natural byproduct of this procedure.
Biggest one since our first test though.
Whatever, it means what you're doing is working, rockstar!
Go, Mac. Now. Do exactly what I told you.
But, it's too soon! I thought we still had a little more time before Earth was supposed to get microwaved or whatever!
This was... something else entirely.
Jude, are you all--
I'm gonna die?
In this lousy century?
Fuck.

But, we just accidentally blew chunks of the future into that time hole!
You recognize where it opened to, right?!
My girl.
I saw the place where I found her.
I wish there was something I could do, but...
Yeah, you can mess with time all you want, but there's no cheating death, huh?
Not like I was destined for a long life anyway.
I thought these monsters worked for you!
A few of the females left this realm to work alongside us...but I have no idea what these natives intend.
Regardless, I think we should get you elsewhere.

You've seen that place before?
I've been there!
You people... you must be who Wari thought was sending her stuff!
Her and her precious boy.
Oh.
Oh, Jesus.
You have the same disease as my...my girlfriend.
The one some time travelers get?
Most travelers by the time my generation rolls around. Lucky if you're immune. Our implants can redirect the mutations for a while...but nothing stops the inevitable.
Our four-dimensional guests first revealed themselves to the world when I was about your age, on the day we all discovered that time travel was possible.
What we call the Editrixes helped us understand the awesome responsibilities that come with--
Bullshit!

Sorry, who's Wari?
An old woman I met a...a long time ago.
No, she's a 12-year-old girl we met in exactly the past you guys have been dumping your mistakes into!
Tiffany, your older self doesn't remember any of your extra-temporal exploits before she encountered you as an adult in the year 2000.
Because all of this trauma will be erased before you and your friends are returned home safely.
I'd forgotten.
I'd forgotten how beautiful it was.
If time travel is pretty much a death sentence, why do you guys do it?
For all the kids who come after us.
And if there's some old piece of tech in your time that might help them down the line, then I...I know what I have to do.
Time travel wasn't "discovered," it was invented... by the woman who raised you!

What the hell did you just say?
Don't... be afraid.
It's not... as scary... as you think.
What isn't?
Do me a favor and don't tell my boyfriend what you know.
It's not like he could stop it, and I...I don't want him to be *sad* for however much time we've got left together.
What the hell did you just say?
That whatever war you've been part of is *stupid*.
I barely understand it, but I still seem to know way more than *you*.

Don't worry, whatever the old-timers are going to do to you--to us--won't hurt a bit.
What do you mean going to do?! I thought all of this was about defeating the old-timers!
Actually, we told you we were going to end the war, not win it.
I promise... it doesn't even... hurt.
Almost feels... exciting?
Wow, you are so not like anyone I've ever met.
That's just the smell of a guy who hasn't bathed in literally decades.
Now let's move before the
strikes back.
Nothing you say makes a lick of sense.
My mother wasn't some inventor, she was--
AAAAHHH!

So my friends and I are getting our brains washed by the bad guys as part of your *surrender?*
This isn't a surrender, it's a *truce.*
One that will last *forever.*
...like something *wonderful...*
...is... about... to...
Come again?
I don't know how you'd translate it, but it's what we call that *blast* you saw back there.
Been happening more and more since we arrived, so just... try not to get killed by the next one, I guess.
CARDINAL!

My friends and I will forget everything that's happened! Everything that's *made* us friends!
I swear, it's a small price to pay for the lifetime of happiness you'll eventually find in this paradise.
You told me the next twelve years of my life will be a *train wreck!* Why do I have to make the same mistakes as you?!
Can I ask one last thing?
Do my boys at least get *revenge* on whatever asshole eventually does me in?
The old-timer who murders you, he...he gets *shot.*
Don't shoot!
It's not trying to hurt her!
We don't know *what* it's doing!

It has to happen this way because it *did* happen this way.
I thought your side was the one that believed history could be *changed.* That if we had the power to go make things better, we *should.*
Now you sound like everything you used to fight *against.*
That's something, I guess.
Is it?
Aren't you sick of all this goddamn *death?*
I'm not losing anyone else!

I guess we *all* grow up to be old-timers, huh?
Spoken like a girl who's seen some shit.
I killed a man.
A *bad* man. In the past. The *way* past. I...I had to. To help save my friends.
BLAM

Um, guys?
Yo, Time Capsule!
Qanta Braunstein has added an authorized guest!
Welcome, authorized guest!
Yeah, that tracks.
As long as there have been young people, there have been older ones forcing us to fight their--
Um, Jude?

Is it finally happening?
Yep.
The last domino's been tipped.
Destination?
Back home.
Ass-crack of the morning on November 1, 1988.
EMERGENCY LAUNCH
OVERRIDE
AFETY PROTOCOLS
00:03
Oh...

NOOoo!
It's a *trap!*
Make it snappy.
KJ, don't!
It's all right.
I've *seen* this before.
...crap.

"Rule #2: A paperboy smokes neither cigarillo nor pipe 'til his work is done."

–From *The American Newspaper Delivery Guild Handbook,* published in 1932

Warning:
AppleX User Terms
and Conditions have
been updated.

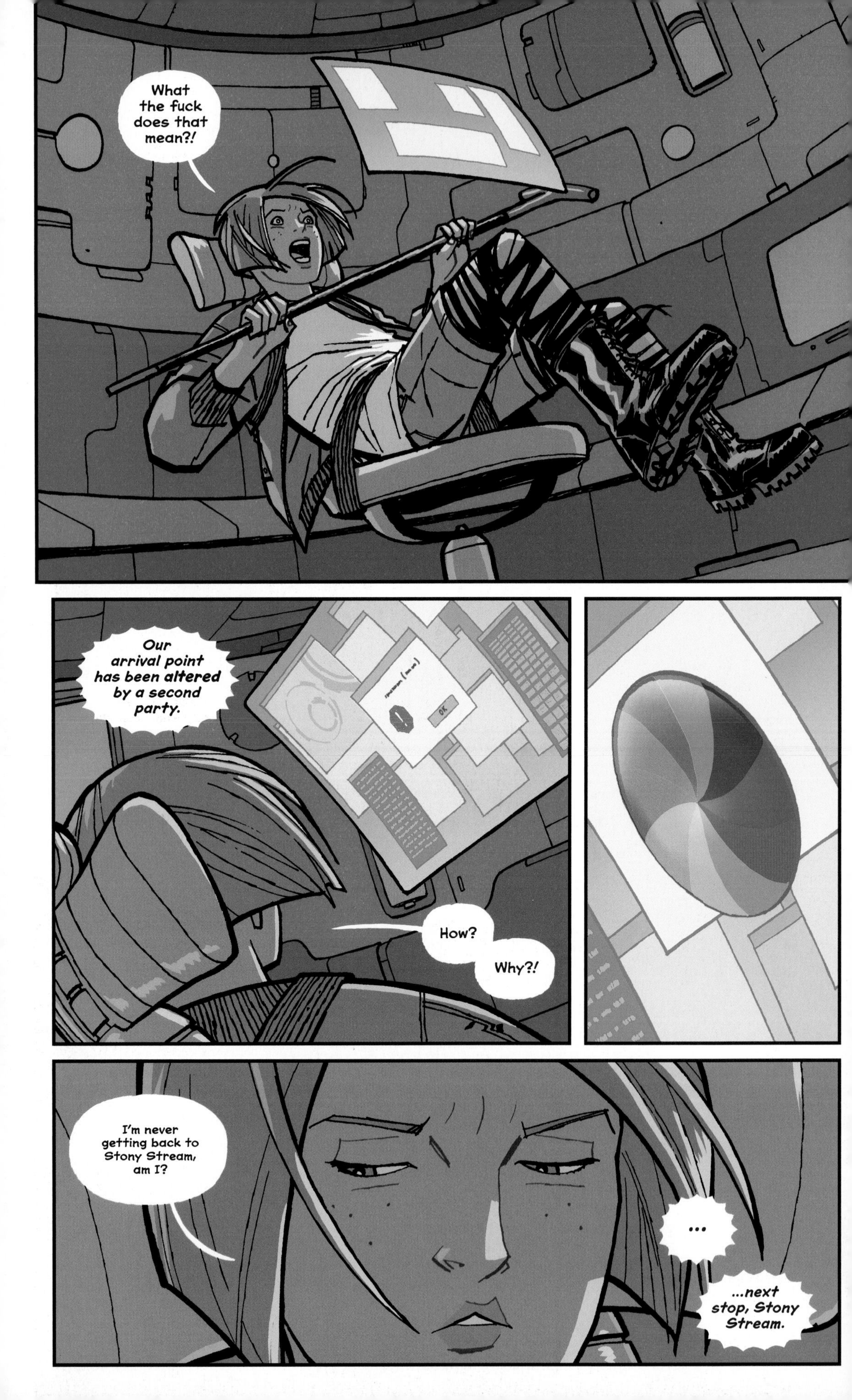
What the fuck does that mean?!
Our arrival point has been altered by a second party.
How?
Why?!
I'm never getting back to Stony Stream, am I?
...
...next stop, Stony Stream.

Come again?

WHUMPF

HNNG!
Error 717: We are approaching the requested geographic destination, but the incorrect temporal designation.

I have other concerns, as well.

Time Capsule, what year is this?
Are there gonna be goddamn **dinosaurs** when I step out there?
Today is Tuesday, August 2, 1831.

But although it is approaching noon, HealthX readings suggest that all inhabitants of this hamlet are ***asleep.***

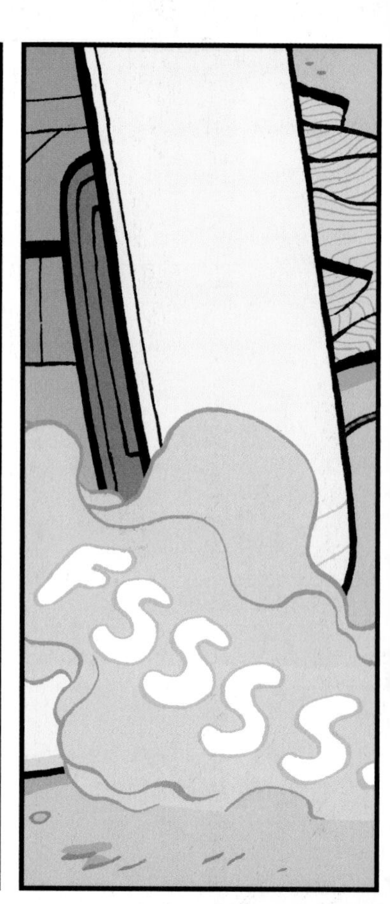
FSSSS

Well, that makes absolutely no sense.

Whatever, how long will it take to get to 1988 from here?
It will take... sorry, remaining battery is reserved for Doctor Braunstein's Last Will & Testament.

Confirmed, delivering to primary beneficiary.
Please stand clear of the closing door.
Hey, no, what are you--

Thank goodness you made it, Mac.

If your bad ass hadn't survived to join us, the entire third dimension would have *shattered* like a...a...

...what do you call the top of a crême brûlée?
What the hell is happening?
Is this a dream?

Nope, that future version of me is *real.*
The bad news is, she and her weird buddies want to *lobotomize* us.

Tiffany!
You're not dead yet!

My team and I didn't come to this neutral ground to *hurt* anyone, but to safely transport you to the same predawn hours of November from which you disappeared.
We just need to...*adjust some memories* before sending you home.

And for what it's worth, just because you'll forget a few days together doesn't mean your experiences didn't really happen.

Which means I'm still going to *bite it,* yeah?

Figured.
It's not fair!
If you've got this higher-than-high tech, why don't we go *way* back, stop us from ever finding that stupid time machine in the first place?
We tried, actually.
Millions and millions of times.

In every attempt to ***retcon*** that stretch of the timestream, the best we could ever do was, like, change the date Mac first met another one of you girls by a few weeks.
The "current" is now so strong at that point in the "stream," it's all but impossible for you four ***not*** to be drawn together into that dank Ohio basement.

That's almost worse than never meeting at all! If all we remember is delivering a few papers, we won't ***stay*** together.
You said it yourself, the four of us ***drift apart*** after that last Hell Morning.
You've learned what Newton said about every action, right?
P

Besides, you're ***twelve.***
No matter what happens next, you'll make plenty of ***new--***
How did I not notice it?

You're...you're ***her,*** aren't you? Only, old and stuff?

Not exactly, Ms. Coyle.
I'm but a humble, 42-year-old ***clone*** of your friend KJ, created to weather the same kinds of storms as the original article.

Who, by the by, should be ***joining*** us in three...two...

...hello?

Kaje!
Careful.
How can we be sure this isn't another evil mimeograph of her?

Because I know you taste like cigarettes and Ultra Brite toothpaste.

...is that bad?

It's memorable.

What is *wrong* with you kids?
Can't you leave anything well enough alone?!

He's got Erin!
GUN!
Steady on, Old-Timer.
We come in peace...
...but we didn't come *unarmed.*
Peace?
You blew up our Cathedral, killed every last soul aboard!
Actually, *your* actions caused the ship's destruction, but before your people could perish, *we* safely transported all of them back where they belong.
Then why haven't you let us to do the same for *this* girl?!
If she and her companions aren't deposited back in their era shortly, all of space and time will fracture like...like...
Yeah, crème brûlée, we heard.
And we know what needs to be done, Grand Father.
But first, we need something from *you.*

We're not just papergirls, we're friends.
The heck do you keep saying, Tiff?
A Hail Mary?

Kind of.
*We're not just papergirls, we're **friends**.*
We're not just papergirls...

Whatever it is, ***no***.
After all the friends I lost on C-Day, I won't negotiate with terrorists, not even when the very continuum is on the line.

This isn't a negotiation, it's a ***blood oath.***
If your generation will agree to the immediate and permanent cessation of ***all*** nonstandard movement through four-dimensional space...then so will ours.

But.
You're talking about the end of time travel.

Forever and ever, amen.
Obviously, we can't prevent whatever excursions have ***already*** taken place along the line, but together, we can ensure that this power is never exploited again.
Listen to her!

Don't you want this stupid war to ***end?***

I do.
Which is why I've fallen for empty gestures from our descendants before.

I'm sorry.

So are we.
Because we didn't just pluck *you* from the next dimension over.
eh?

How... how dare you!
How dare you turn them against me!
You **shot** one of their friends!

I was trying to **protect** you!
That's all we "old-timers" **ever** tried to do for you ungrateful shits!

Why do you think these creatures **picked** me for this godforsaken life?
Because I--

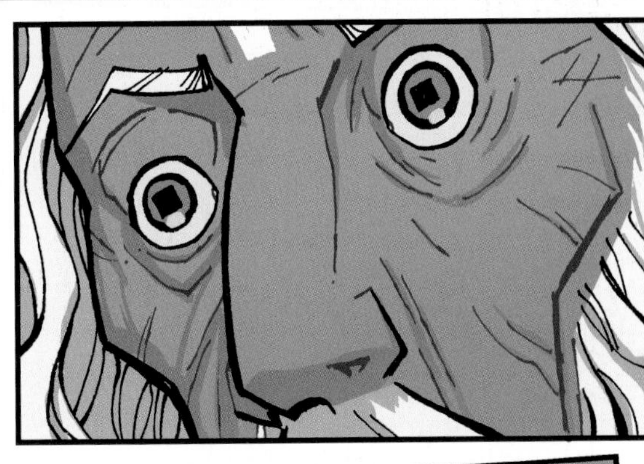

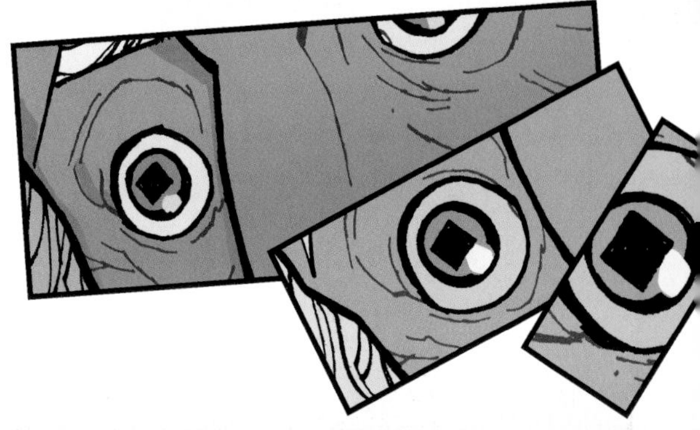

WATCH
NEEDZ U!
NG GORENG

I'll be damned.

I am...
...not the man I thought I was.

The Stones were wrong.
Time isn't on *anyone's* side, is it?

For what it's worth, took *us* thousands of years to finally learn that lesson.
Hhn.
Your terms.
I *agree.*

That's it?
No epic final battle?
Can you please sound less disappointed?

Does that mean we get to go home?

You'll each be safely deposited back in your lives, in the early hours shortly *after* you originally found the time machine, events you'll no longer recall.
I vaguely remember waking up *late* for my route that day, which I blamed on some crazy-vivid nightmares I instantly forgot.

I know it sounds like a lot, but removing all of the trauma you were exposed to is actually the *least* we can do.

Trauma? This has been the best time of my life!
I *rode* a gigantic microscopic bug! Like at a *rodeo!*

Yeah, why can't we just hold onto the good stuff?

Like my cool new boots.
I hate you.

Unfortunately, this is a package deal.
Anything you picked up during your travels has to stay behind, including what's in here.

It's for the best, girls.
One of you *took a life*, and while that may not weigh on her yet, I promise it would over time.

She'd come to dwell not just on the man she was forced to end, but on all of the *descendants* she likely helped erase from history.

Believe me, endless branches of their possible faces will haunt her for the rest of--
Enough!

I vote we get on with the brainwashing already.

Mac, are you sure?
No.
But at least I'll go back to not really believing that I'm gonna *die* someday.
That'll feel nice, right?
And who knows?
Even if the four of us are destined to lose touch, at least we'll have--

Apologies, but time is of the essence.

I...I didn't even get to say goodbye!

And all that pain you're feeling is about to disappear, too.

We're not just papergirls, we're--

WAIT!

What Eve did!
In the Garden of Eden!
I...I don't think it was evil.

It was smart.
It was *right.*

Does anyone know what the hell she's talking about?
The mythical first woman.
From their Bible?

Don't worry, beautiful.
That's just another silly old story...

...written by a bunch of dudes.

"Rule #1: A paperboy treats every other paperboy as his brother."

–From *The American Newspaper Delivery Guild Handbook,* published in 1932

If you laugh at me, I'm gonna punch you in the boob.
KJ
Karina

Jesus.

Pretty much the opposite.
KJ, you look...
I mean, I didn't know this was gonna be so... dressy.

Relax, it's not *your* bat mitzvah.
Am I the only kid not from your school here?
Sorry I'm late!

This stupid thing got stuck in my *spokes.*

New kid!
Mac, you've known me for almost a *year.*

How come you don't just call me by my real name?

Because I...I have no idea what it is.
Neither do I, actually.
When did we meet again?

You guys, listen to me.
It's super, super important that you *don't forget* what I'm about to--

GUN!

Hey.
Y LOGGING:
5 65311
9 10930
75 76 75744
65 21 12025
53 78 10690
Tiff?
What are you--
RRIDE MULTIPLE TARGETS
SSESSMENT: POTENTIAL DO
EMBER NUMBER: 3905137
See you real soon.
ERIN!
snap
That was her name.

I have a message.
Please.
You have to dance with me.
Like, slow dance?
Remember.
We're not just papergirls. We're--
Mac, you love me.
I do?
I--
DUDE!

Mmf?
You overslept, stupid.
...time is it?
Like, five something.

Oh, shit.
It's Hell Morning.
And my boys are still out there, so I hope you're ready to get egged in the *face.*

Is Dad home yet?
I doubt it.
Why?
'Cause I could use a hand rubber-banding my stack.
Don't look at me.
Ain't my route anymore.
Cool jacket, butch.
Goddammit.
What now?
I can't fall asleep without James and Lars!
Where the hell's my Walkman?
Beats me.
Delicious PIZZA
Thank You

WOMEN
for
BUSH
88

Karina?

Aren't you late for your little job, sweetheart?
Oh.
Yeah, thanks, Mom.
I would have woken you up sooner, but it looked like you were having the sweetest dream of all time.

I kind of was, actually.
It was sometime in the *future*, and my friends and I were all at this amazing party, and... and...
CAMP

...shoot.

It's gone.

PRESS START TO CONTINUE

...not... just... paper...

ROUND
36
Round 36.
Another fifteen minutes, and I could probably *beat* it, or at least figure out a way to...

ARKANOID

What is *wrong* with you?
ESS START
CONTINUE
ROUND 36

ROUND 36

Nintendo
ENTERTAINMENT SYSTEM
POWER
RESET

KERRASH
The heck?
MONSTER SQUAD
Sorry, Missy.
My alarm must not have gone off, and if I don't hurry--
What's on your stomach?
My...?

Huh.
Erin, did you get a *tattoo?*
It's not a tattoo, it's more like a... *rash.*

I've never seen one like *that.*
Yeah, well, you don't even know what puberty is.
All sorts of weird stuff starts happening to your--

I'm telling Mom.

Missy, please.
If you do that, she's not going to let me make my rounds, and the *Preserver* will *fire* me.
So what? It's not like you have to pay for your own food or clothes or anything! Why do you need this so bad?

You'll understand when you're older.

Mac!

How's it going?
Say again?
Don't know if you remember, but we delivered together last year.

Tonya, right?
Tiffany.
Anyway, the psychos are still out in full effect. You want to team up again?

Maybe.
Have you, *uh,* seen ***KJ*** tonight?

Not yet.
But I ran into some new deliverer named Erin.
Is he a dork?

She seemed all right to me.

Erin with an "E"? For real?
How many of us are working Stony Stream now?

Guess you started a fad.
Hnn.
Where's the new kid now?

Over in the evergreen streets.
Told her to give me a call if anything comes up.

Give you a call *how?* The nearest payphone is like a *mile* from here.
The Cleveland Preserver

Welcome to the future.
P

A walkie-talkie?
Hardly.
This is a Realistic TRC-218 CB with channel--
kzzt Um, calling Tiffany? kzzt

It's me, the girl you gave this thing to? Um, over? kzzt
Definitely a dork.

What's up, Erin?
I don't know yet, exactly. I...I didn't know if I should follow them by myself or what.

But I saw three creepy guys in costumes follow **another** papergirl down that cul-de-sac at the end of Hemlock...and she hasn't come out yet.

Over.

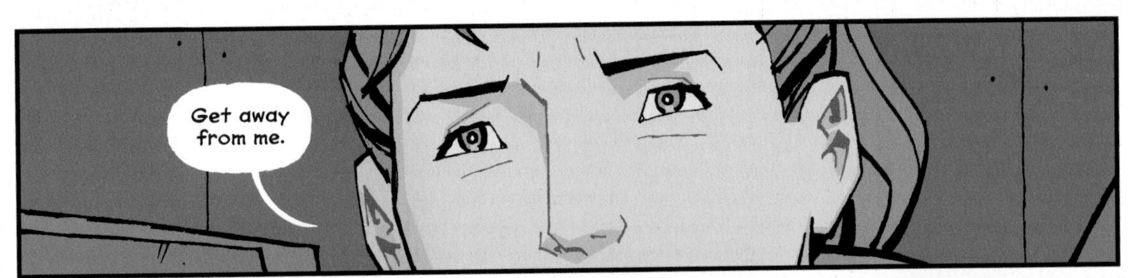
Get away from me.

Relax, we just wanted to meet the new chick.
Yeah, I didn't recognize those legs.
You go to St. Nick's or St. Pete's?

Neither.
I'm...I'm at Buttonwood.
Thought I smelled academy.

Tell me something.
Is it true what they say about Jewish girls?
Lucas Kurzenberger!

Cool costume, you...
...you...

...fart-
mouth.

What did you just call me?
Trust me, she's said way worse.

And she's not wrong.
Yeah, a little Listermint wouldn't kill you.
Why don't you mind your business, Coyle?

That's exactly what I'm doing, unlike *your* unemployed ass.
My brother told me you got fired from Friendly's for dipping your hairy balls in the Fribble machine.

Hffh.
Ha ha.
Good luck getting home alive, bitch.

I could have handled them on my own, you know.

You're welcome?
KJ, this is Erin.
It's great to meet you, *all* of you. I just wanted to say, I'm so impressed by--

There are more of those dipshits out there.
We should keep moving.
I was thinking we could split up into two groups, finish the development faster?
Or?

Because of the evil high schoolers and stuff?
Maybe all four us could maybe...stick together?

Just an idea.

ARRRRRR...OOOOOOO

ROOOO

What's with these dweebs?
I outgrew trick-or-treating when I was *eight*.
Who'd you go as, Tiff?

I don't know, either an astronaut or the devil.
How about you guys?

Probably Annie.
I was **obsessed** with that movie when it came out.
Yeah, I dressed up as Miss Hannigan that year.

The bad guy?!
But, you didn't even need a wig to be the hero!
Annie is fine and all, but Hannigan is a total **badass.** There's a **reason** she gets invited to the White House at the end of the...

Whatever, it's stupid.

Back in '83, I dressed up as Robin. From Batman? But I got scared looking out my window at all the neighborhood kids and went to hide under my parents' bed.
I ended up getting a fever and didn't go out, and that was pretty much it for my mom and dad, so I never went out on Halloween again.

That is the single saddest story I've heard in my entire life.
HONK
HONK

Go around, asshole!

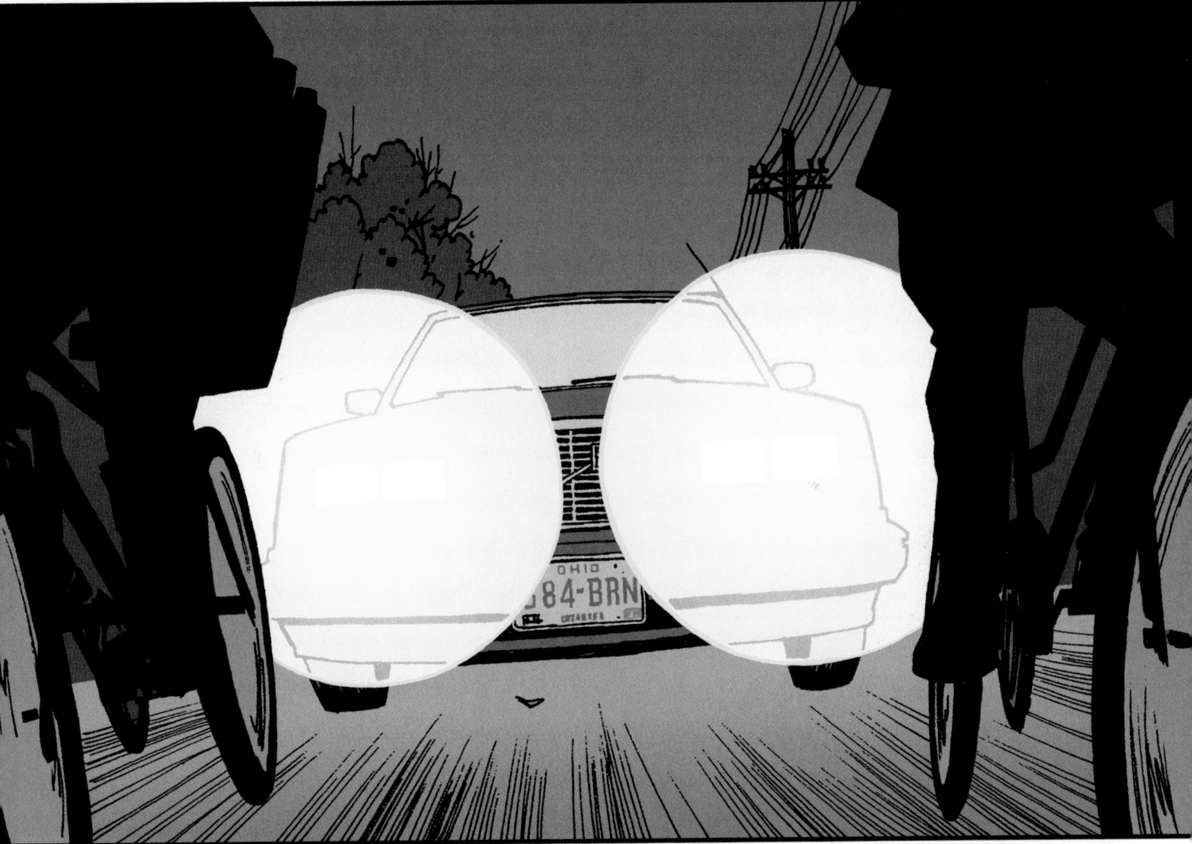

Ah, man.
Not the station wagon again.

This guy has bothered you before?
Lady, actually.
A few days ago, I think she tried following me, and I had to--
STOP
SSSCREE

eerrrrrrrrrrrrrrrrrrrrrr
OHIO
884-BRN
errrrrrrrrrrrrrrrrrrrrrrt
884-BRN
Uhff.

Are you all right?!
What the hell, lady?!
You could have--

OHIO
254 AXY
CUYAHOGA

Eff me.
If...if we had crossed that intersection...
STOP

STOP
VRRRRRRRRRRRRR

WAIT!

Who are you?!

What's it matter?
I'm just glad the drunk idiot almost hit us when she did.
But, what if it *wasn't* an accident?

What if that was, like... our guardian angel?

flic
You know *Highway to Heaven* is fake, right?
Ah, Mac.

May I have a cigarette?

Please...?

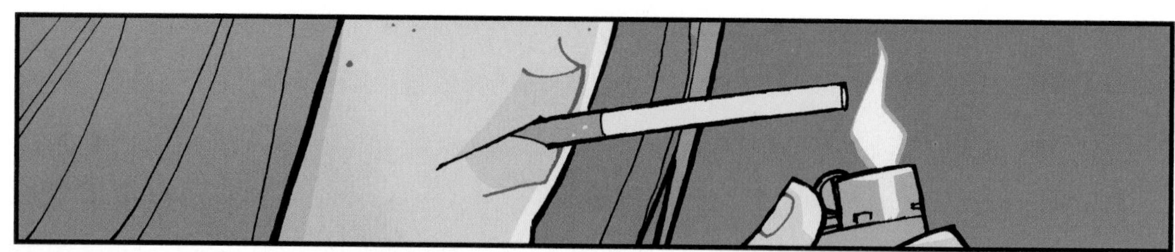

Hhhh.
With all the warnings and stuff, I didn't think it was gonna *taste* so great.
Good ol' forbidden fruit.

koff
But, aren't you worried about ***dying?***
Not as worried as I am about living a life that isn't fuckin' awesome.

I think I'm going to quit.

You only started three puffs ago!
Not smoking, ***delivering.***
I'm pretty sure my papergirl days are done.

Why, Tiffany?
Don't get me wrong, I loved this job.
I never thought I'd be able to knock on complete strangers' doors and tell them to *pay* me. And I started doing that shit when I was eleven years old!

But these days, it's kind of become *only* about the money.

And what's wrong with that?
Hey, I've been able to buy myself more stuff than I ever could have imagined... but it's still *stuff.*

And most of whatever I *think* I'll like is just some slightly different version of crap that made me feel happy when I was a kid.
I mean, maybe I need to grow up a little?

So quitting a paying job is more "grown up" than having one?
Yeah, what are you ever gonna do that will be better than this?

I don't want to *do* anything, I just want to...*be.*
At least for a little while.

And you know when your last morning will be and every-thing?
I was kind of thinking I'd turn my bag over to the *Preserver* **today.**
If you three would be willing to pick up my customers?
Jackpot.
Yeah, thank you so much.
But, don't you still have a few last porches left?
Down to my final four.
Then let's get to it.
I mean, our handbook clearly says, "A paperboy always finishes strong."
Have you looked around?
Paperboys went extinct.
tsssssss

WHAPF

Can't believe you're *retiring* that beautiful arm.
I'm serious, you should really think about lacrosse.
Heh, maybe.

Is that the goddamn sun coming out already?
Stupid day-light savings, messes me up every year.
I don't know, I kind of *like* it.

Especially in the fall, when we get a whole extra hour.
Sometimes, I'll stay awake until three in the morning, just so I can, you know, experience those same sixty minutes *twice.*

Why?
...
I have no idea.

Well.
This has been real, but I should be getting home.
Same here.
Maybe we'll do this again next year, new kid.
Yeah, maybe so.
And I'll probably still see you around the neighborhood, right?
Almost definitely.
Okay then.
Catch you freaks later.
STOP

Later.

See ya!

Bye.

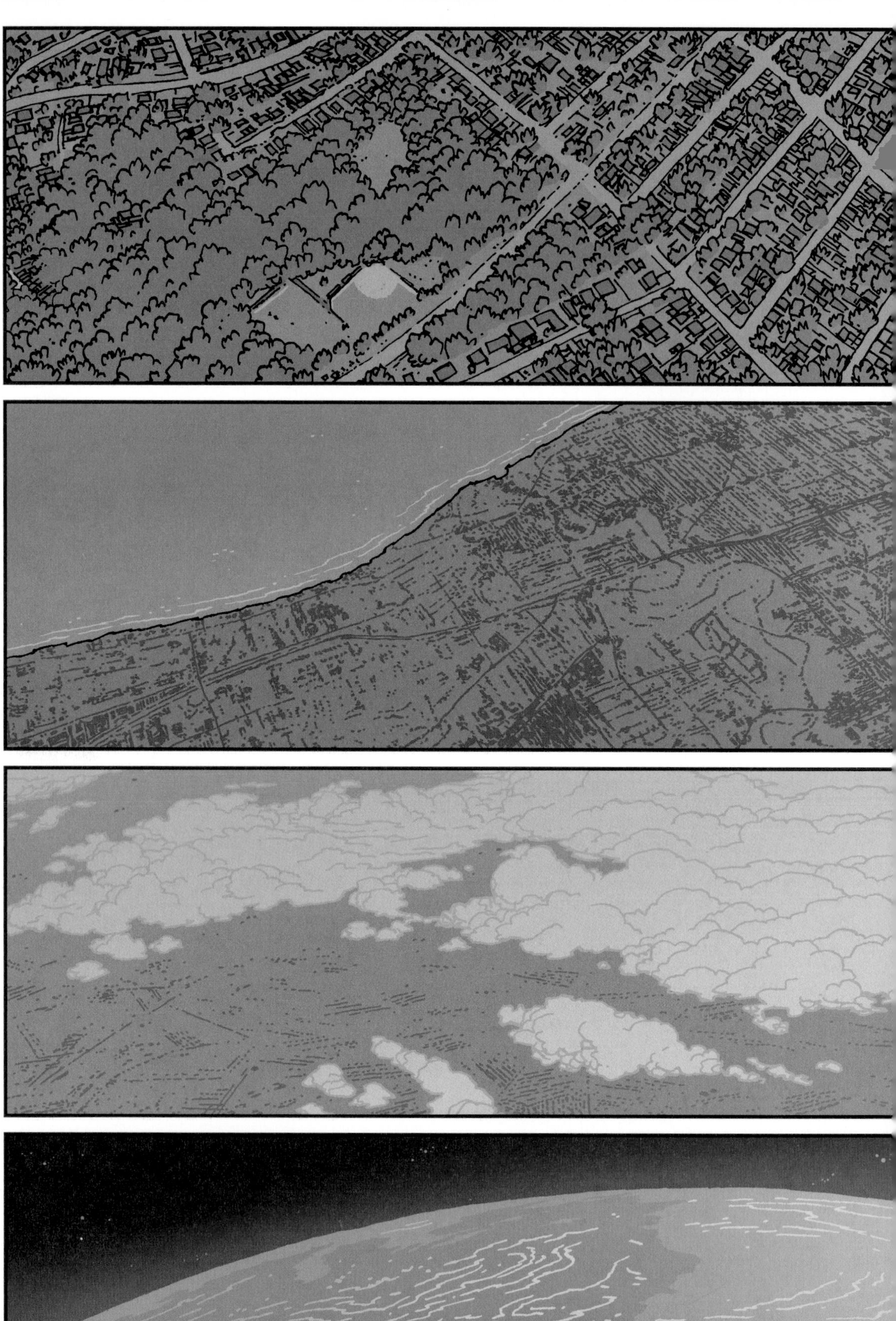
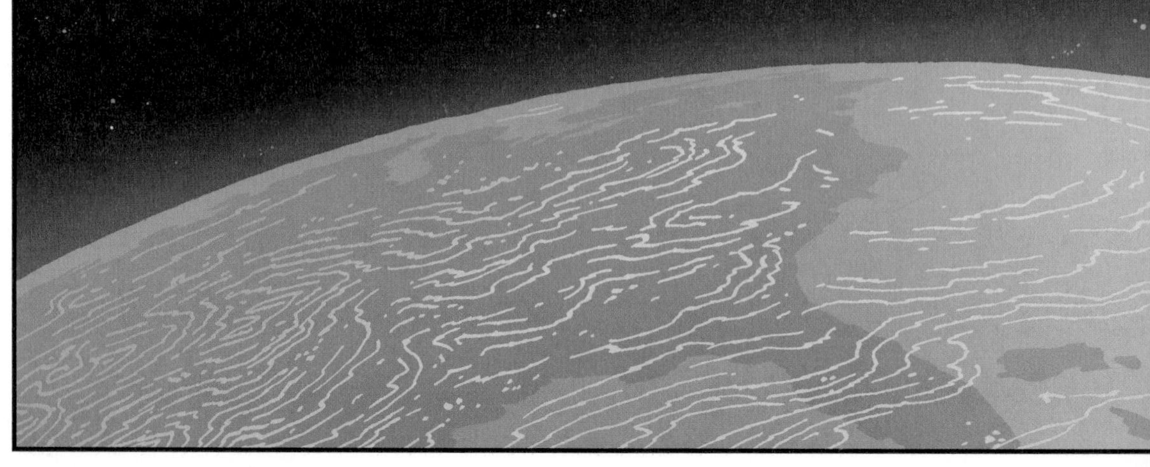

Wait!

You guys!
Hold up!

Hey.
Um, I'm not sure about you, but I don't have to start getting ready for school for, like, another hour.

Want to ride together a little longer?

...sure.

Why not?
Yeah, I'm in.

Cool.

fump

Ow.
What was that for?
Yellow punch buggy.

No punch backs.